S0-AWX-355

Red or Blue, I Like You!

By Sarah Albee

Illustrated by Tom Brannon

Dalmatian Press, LLC, 2005. All rights reserved.
Published by Dalmatian Press, LLC, 2005. The DALMATIAN PRESS name and logo are trademarks of Dalmatian Press, LLC, Franklin, Tennessee 37067. No part of this book may be reproduced or copied in any form without written permission from the copyright owner.

Printed in the U.S.A.
ISBN: 1-40371-045-7 (X) 1-40371-352-9 (M)

06 07 08 LBM 10 9 8 7 6 5 4
13806 Sesame Street: Red or Blue, I Like You!

One day in the dentist's waiting room, Elmo made a new friend. Her name was Angela.

When it was time for Angela to go in for her checkup, she asked her father, "Can Elmo come over to our house to play tomorrow?"

Angela's father glanced at Elmo's mother, who smiled and nodded.

The next day, Elmo's mother brought Elmo to Angela's house. When Elmo got there, he couldn't stop looking around Angela's neigborhood.

"Um, Angela?" asked Elmo. "How come all the
monsters in your neighborhood are blue? Where are all the
different-colored monsters we have on Sesame Street?"

"I don't know." Angela shrugged. "Come on inside!
I'll show you my room!"

Elmo and Angela were playing with Angela's train set when her brother, Tony, walked in with some of his friends.

"Hey," Tony said, "do you guys want to come watch *Supermonster* with us?"

"No, thanks," Elmo and Angela said at the same time.

"I thought all red monsters *loved* that show!" Tony said.

"No," said Elmo. "Elmo prefers to play with trains."

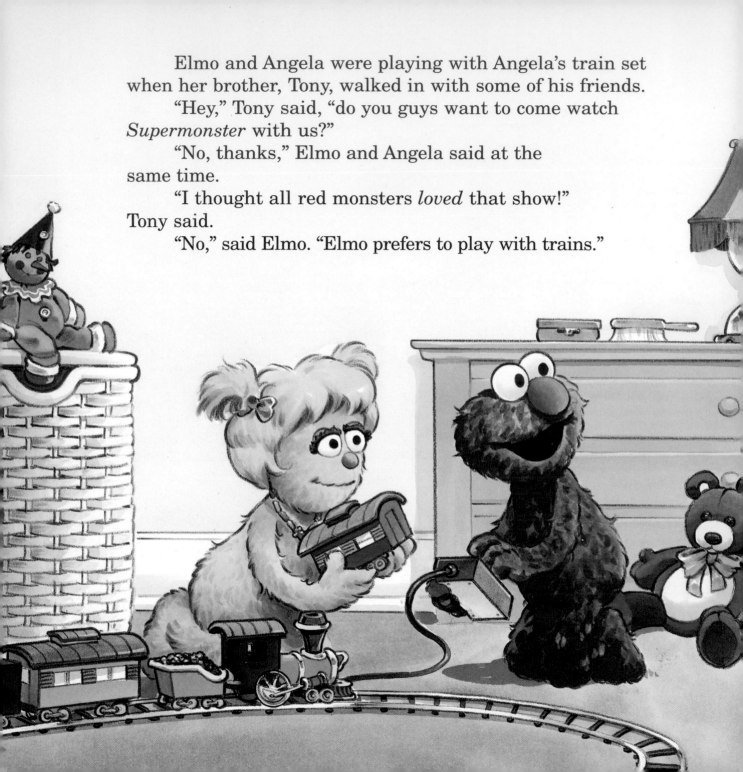

"I hope you like spaghetti, Elmo!"
said Angela's mother at lunch time.

"It's Elmo's favorite," said Elmo.

"So you red monsters like a lot of the same
stuff we blue monsters do, huh?" asked Tony.
"I thought all red monsters liked to eat was,
you know, red-monster food."

"Red monsters like all kinds of food,"
said Elmo. "Except maybe brussels sprouts."

Elmo's mother came to pick him up.

"Can Angela come over to Elmo's house tomorrow?"
Elmo asked her.

"Well, we'll be having our family reunion. But she is
welcome to come!" his mother replied.

So the next day, Angela went to Elmo's house.

"Hi, Angela!" said Elmo. But Angela wasn't looking at Elmo. She was looking all around.

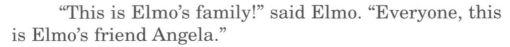

"This is Elmo's family!" said Elmo. "Everyone, this is Elmo's friend Angela."

"Hi," said Angela in a small voice.

"Hello, Angela," said Elmo's aunt. "Elmo says you love spaghetti, so we will make some especially for you."

"But I like chicken and fruit salad, too," said Angela, pointing at the food on the table.

"Oh!" said Elmo's aunt. "I didn't realize that blue monsters liked that kind of food."

While they were eating, there was a knock at the door, and Zoe came in. "Hi, Elmo!" she said. "I'm just dropping off the book I borrowed."

"She's orange, just like your aunt," said Angela after Zoe had left.

"Mmm-hmm," said Elmo.

Then Telly popped in. "We're having a T-ball game,
Elmo!" he said. "Come on out and play!"

"He's pink," whispered Angela.

"Yup," said Elmo. "Come on, let's go play!"

As they walked down Sesame Street, Angela kept looking around. "Wow," she said. "There are all different-colored monsters around here!"

"And birds and grouches and people and some Snuffleupaguses, too!" Elmo said. "And we all live happily together."

Angela played T-ball with Elmo and all
of his friends. She hit a home run.

"Hey, everyone!" called Big Bird, running into the park. "There's a new family moving in across the street! Let's all go welcome them to Sesame Street!"

Both teams dropped their gloves and hurried after Big Bird.

"Wow," said Angela. "This is one cool street you live on, Elmo. Can I come back and play tomorrow?"

"Oh, sure, Angela," Elmo replied. "You can come back anytime! All monsters are always welcome on Sesame Street!"